To Linda, Brian and Sarah Robinson,
and to Gordon Bult, who is always in charge

First published in Great Britain in 2003 by Bloomsbury Publishing Plc
38 Soho Square, London, W1D 3HB

A CIP catalogue record of this book is available from the British Library
ISBN 0 7475 6199 0

Designed by Tracey Cunnell

Printed in Hong Kong/China

1 3 5 7 9 10 8 6 4 2

Gordon in Charge

By Jill Newton

Gordon was a bossy goat and thought
he was in charge of the farm.

When Gordon gave orders the other
animals obeyed (for a quiet life).

'Heads down, and CHEW! Keep in line,
you scruffy bunch of sheep!

You cows! Stop larking about and MOO
in tune this time!

One, two, three and LAY those eggs, hens!
I want a dozen by lunchtime!'

Then early one morning, a new arrival waddled into the yard.

'Who are you?'
demanded Gordon the goat.

'I am Gordon
the goose,'
said Gordon
the goose.

Gordon the goat blinked. 'I really don't think so. I'm afraid you will have to change your name. I am Gordon – and I am in charge!'

'No, no, no,' laughed the goose. 'My name is Gordon. I'd be much better at keeping this lot in order than you, and I'll prove it.

You see the pond behind the barn?' he continued. 'If I swim across it faster than you then I am Gordon and I should be in charge.'

‘I think not,’ said Gordon the goat, running after Gordon the goose who was already jumping into the water.

'There *you* go!' exclaimed the goose.
'**I** can swim faster, so **I'm** in charge.'
'That's not fair!' bleated the soggy goat.

'You see that gate next to the path?' he asked.
'If I push it over before *you* that will *mean* that
I am Gordon and **I** am in charge.'

And hurtling towards the gate with his head down, it took Gordon the goat just one butt to knock it flying...

along with the goose.

'That's not fair!' honked Gordon the goose. 'You didn't say 'go'. I have a better idea.

You see those roses by the house? The one who picks the most can be Gordon **and** in charge.'

With a flurry of petals and leaves, both Gordons emerged from the former rosebed with mouthfuls of flowers.

All the other animals were watching by now, enjoying the entertainment and enjoying not being bossed about.

Cow counted up the flowers.
It was a dead heat.
'Recount!' demanded the Gordons.
So Sheep counted,
then Pig counted, but it was still equal.

'OK,' said Gordon the goat.
'This will decide it.

First one to the top of the barn can be Gordon. First one to the top is in charge.'
'Easy-peasy,' honked Gordon the goose.

They climbed and flew and scrabbled
and fluttered and both reached the top
of the roof ... at the same time.
'I was here first!'

'No! I was here first!'

'Who was here first?' they yelled at the animals down below.

A long,

long way

down

below.

The goat felt wobbly. The goose felt dizzy. They stopped yelling. Neither of them knew how to get down. They were stuck on the roof and felt scared.

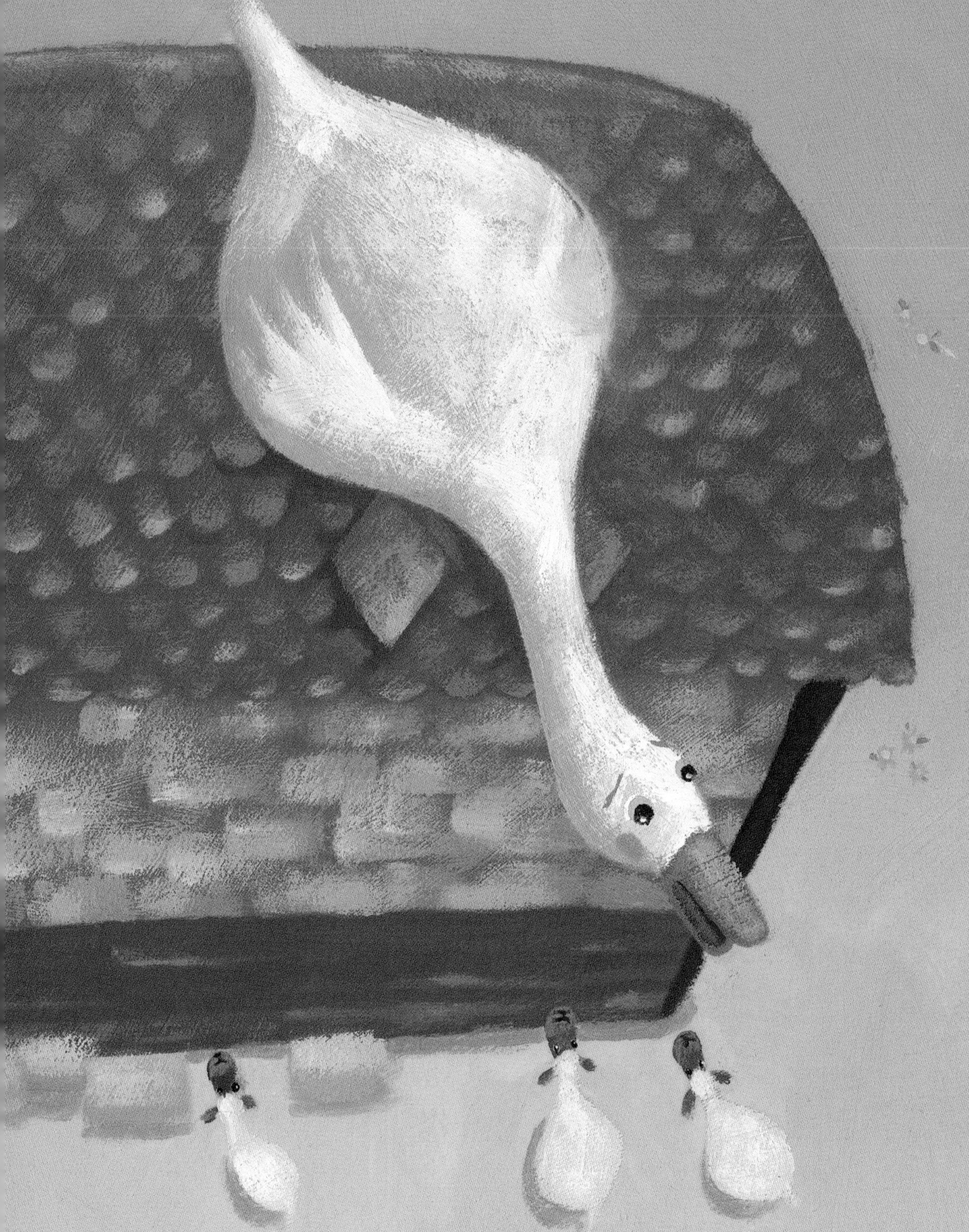

'Help!

Help!'

they honked and bleated together.

A ladder appeared, followed
by a big beardy face.
'Well, well. What on earth are
you two doing?' it said.

'We're Gordon and we're in charge,' said the two rather sheepish looking creatures.

The big beardy face blinked. 'I really don't think so. I am Gordon and I am in charge,' said the farmer. And lifting the goose under one arm and the goat under the other, he carried the exhausted animals down the ladder and into the barn.

They had worn each other out.
'I'm very tired,' said the goose.
'I'm very tired too,' said the goat.
'Tired of being in charge,' they agreed.

They looked at each other, surprised.
Agreeing was easy – and seemed quite a lot safer.

So Gordon the goat and Gordon the goose agreed that they were happy for Gordon the farmer to be in charge...

for now...